# Pine and the Winter Sparrow

### Retold by
## Alexis York Lumbard

## Illustrated by Beatriz Vidal

### Foreword by Robert Lewis

✦Wisdom Tales✦

*For Sophia and Daniel, with love.*
—Auntie Lex

*A Mary y Susete, cada vez mas cerca.*
—BV

Pine and the Winter Sparrow
Text copyright © 2015 Alexis York Lumbard, Illustrations copyright © 2015 Beatriz Vidal
All rights reserved. No part of this book may be used or reproduced
in any manner without written permission, except in critical articles and reviews.
Book Design by Stephen Williams.
Wisdom Tales is an imprint of World Wisdom, Inc.

Library of Congress Cataloging-in-Publication Data

Lumbard, Alexis York, 1981-
  Pine and the winter sparrow / retold by Alexis York Lumbard ; illustrated by Beatriz Vidal ;
foreword by Robert Lewis.
     pages cm
  Summary: "Have you ever wondered why pine trees stay green all winter long and don't lose
their leaves like other trees? According to an ancient legend attributed to the Cherokee Indians, it
was a simple act of kindness towards an injured little bird that earned pine trees this very honor.
Retold by award-winning author Alexis York Lumbard, this story invites readers to experience a
world where trees and birds speak and interact with each other, and which shows us that no act of
kindness and sharing goes unrewarded. Featuring beautiful paintings by multiple award-winning
illustrator Beatriz Vidal, you will never look at pine trees in the same way again!"--Provided by
publisher.
  Audience: K to grade 3.
  ISBN 978-1-937786-33-5 (hardcover : acid-free paper)  1.  Cherokee Indians--Folklore. 2.
Pine--Folklore. 3.  Trees--Folklore. 4.  Sparrows--Folklore. 5.  Kindness--Folklore.
[1. Cherokee Indians--Folklore. 2. Indians of North America--Folklore.]  I. Vidal, Beatriz,
illustrator. II. Title.
  E99.C5L885 2015
  398.2089'97557--dc23
                                                                    2014030768

Printed in China on acid-free paper.
Production Date: September 2014, Plant & Location: Printed by 1010
Printing International Ltd,  Job/Batch #: TT14080601
For information address
Wisdom Tales, P.O. Box 2682,
Bloomington, Indiana 47402-2682
www.wisdomtalespress.com

# Foreword

The joy of telling a story is to turn a timeless tale into a living, breathing experience for an audience. Being a storyteller has allowed me this unique privilege. Now Alexis York Lumbard and Beatriz Vidal have transformed an ancient story into words and art—into a poetic experience.

With the opening of *Pine and the Winter Sparrow* you are traveling into a distant moment once spoken under the very same stars we walk amongst. Nature has always been sacred to the indigenous tribes of the Americas: nature is a living, breathing entity. The earth, the sky, all of the animals and birds and peoples are sacred, and learning to think and believe in this native way is learning to see the world through native eyes.

This ancient tale, I believe, inspired the delight of Alexis York Lumbard, evolving into the book you now hold. Alexis has captured the essence of the native spirit in her prose. She and Beatriz Vidal have caught this story's echo with a wonderful rhythm of color and words so quiet and evocative as to take the breath of one reading away into that distant memory of tales told by generations of storytellers. Filled with Beatriz's delicate hues and carried by Alexis' words, you too may become your own storyteller.

Enjoy,
Robert Lewis
Cherokee, Navaho, and Apache storyteller

Each morning Sparrow greeted the Creator with a joyful song. He did so even on the day he injured his wing.

"But winter is coming!" said his family. "And you can hardly fly." "Don't you worry," he chirped. "I'll find a way to carry on."

Autumn had come to an end. Sparrow watched as his family flew south without him. "Until spring my loves. Farewell."

In the passing days, the wintery winds blew fiercer and fiercer. Poor Sparrow shivered and shook. But not Oak. Oak stood tall and still. "Excuse me," said Sparrow. "Would you kindly shelter me? I wish to heal my wing and greet my family come spring."

Oak huffed and puffed. Then he huffed and puffed some more. Finally he grumbled, "Go away little fellow. Go bother someone else."

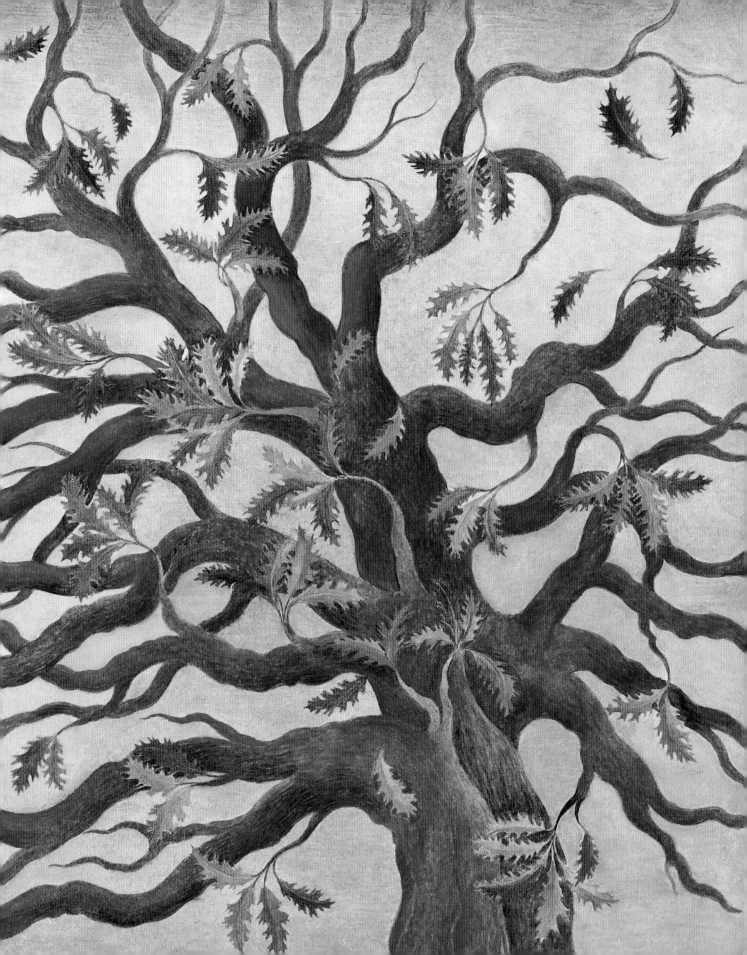

Sparrow skipped to Maple. Her leaves shimmered in the sun like a golden shield. "Good day Maple. *Tweet, tweet.* Might you lend me this one branch from now till winter ends?"

Maple scoffed, "Spend all winter long with you! I think not!" and she twisted her trunk the other way.

Next Sparrow hopped towards Elm. *Tweet. Tweet. Tweet?* But Elm quickly thundered, "Not now. Not ever. Never!"

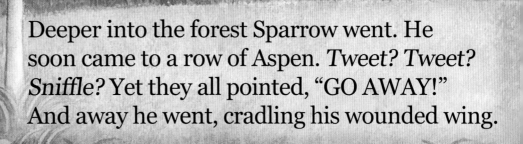

Deeper into the forest Sparrow went. He
soon came to a row of Aspen. *Tweet? Tweet?*
*Sniffle?* Yet they all pointed, "GO AWAY!"
And away he went, cradling his wounded wing.

Sparrow hobbled on . . . and on . . .
until he hobbled to the very edge of the forest. A
flurry of snow drifted down from above. Thoughts
of Sparrow's faraway family tugged at his tiny
heart. With a deep song of sorrow Sparrow wept.

"What's the matter, little bird?" asked a quiet voice. Sparrow looked up. *Sniffle. Sniffle.* SIGH. Pine smiled down. Feeling safe, Sparrow told Pine all his worries.

"Well," said Pine. "If you don't mind my sticky branches and my needle-sharp leaves, then all that I am and all that I have is yours."

Before Sparrow could reply, Pine scooped him up and placed him high on a branch.

Spring returned to the forest and with
its return came Sparrow's family.

"Your wing!" they cheered. "It's all better."
"Yes," said Sparrow, "All thanks to Pine. He
is my very best friend." Pine beamed.

Soon after, the Creator called a council. "Trees of the forest,"
He spoke.

"Those of you who have so much shared nothing. But the one who had so little shared everything. Pine, your gift to Sparrow was a gift to Me. So you alone will remain green against the snow, evergreen evermore."

And that, say the old storytellers, is why all the trees lose their leaves each winter, all except Pine.

# Author's Note

Some of my fondest childhood memories are of playing in the forest of Northern Virginia. I would spend hours collecting twigs and exploring our creek. These days, I often find myself returning to the forest in the stories I read and write.

When I stumbled upon the fable *Why the Trees Lose Their Leaves* in an old collection of Native American stories, I knew it was a gem. Since it was attributed to the Cherokee, I contacted the nation through their official government website, www.cherokee.org, to discover more. I then heard back from their community and school specialist, Robert Lewis. Robert is also a talented storyteller who studied with the late Hastings Shade. He was familiar with a different version of *Why the Trees Lose Their Leaves* and said that the version I read may or may not be Cherokee. In our conversations Robert recalled that "the tribes in the southeast all had somewhat similar tales," and that these tales were often passed from one tribe to another.

It might be that among some of the old-time storytellers, questions of authorship and origin were less significant when compared with the story itself. Stories have a way of caring for us—much like the forest. Maybe this is the reason people shared stories with those who had need of them. I, for one, need stories. Perhaps you do too.

I hope you enjoy *Pine and the Winter Sparrow*, a story inspired by the above tale and the quiet strolls I still enjoy through the forest.

With my thanks to all native storytellers past and present, and especially to Robert Lewis.

Alexis York Lumbard